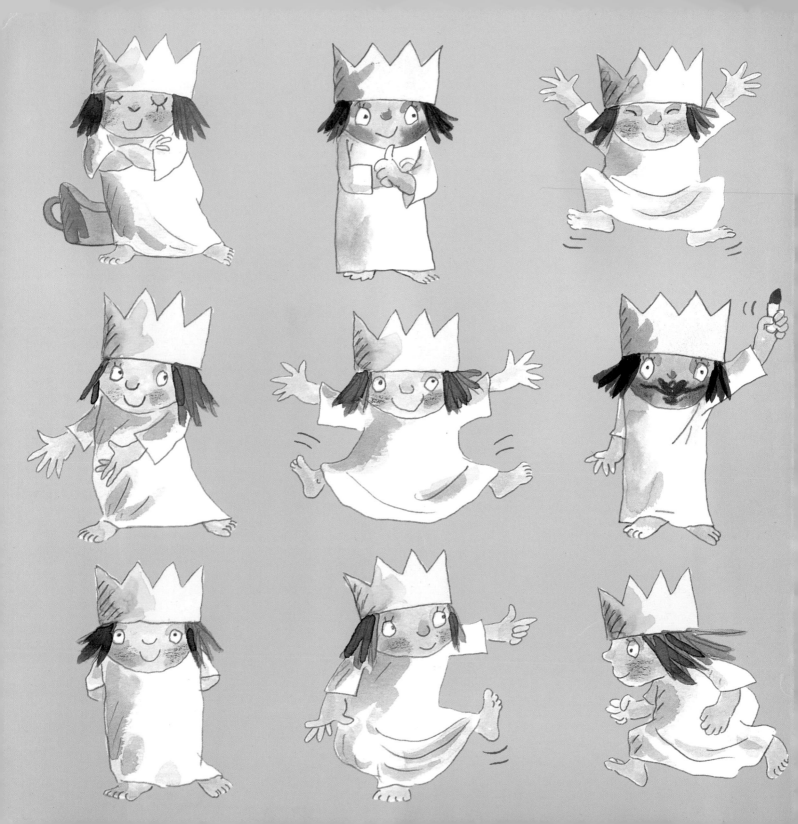

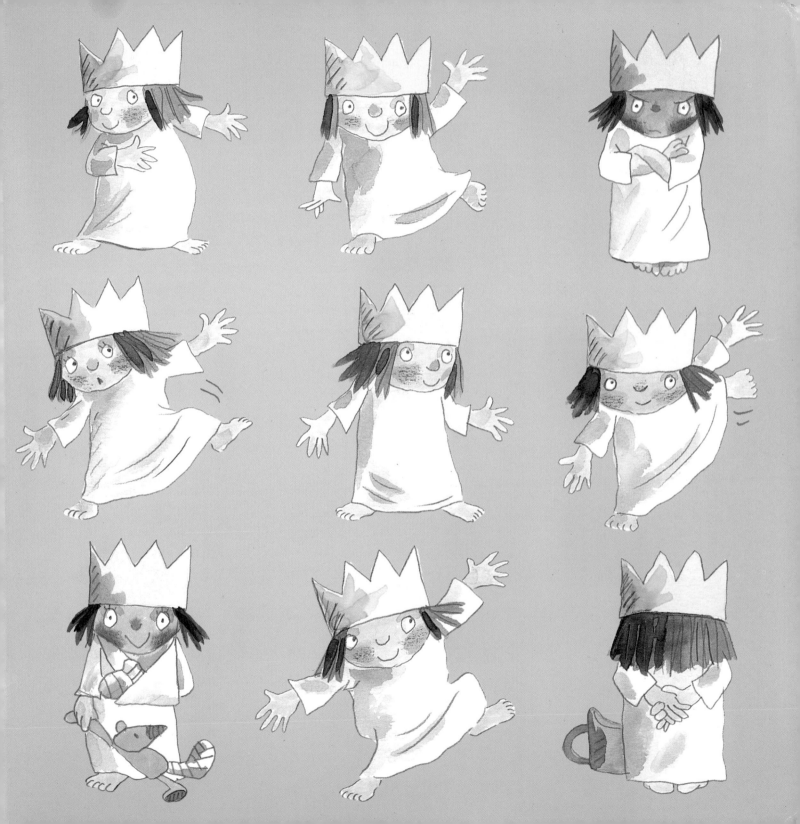

*With my thanks to San Kiu Lieu and Samantha Riches
who gave me the idea for this story and their
permission to use it when they were at
Keyworth Primary School in London*

This edition produced for The Book People Ltd,
Hall Wood Avenue, Haydock, St Helens WA11 9UL

First published in hardback in Great Britain by Andersen Press Ltd in 1999
First published in paperback by Picture Lions in 2000
This edition published by Collins Picture Books in 2001

3 5 7 9 10 8 6 4

ISBN: 0-00-766639-X

Picture Lions and Collins Picture Books are imprints of the Children's Division, part of HarperCollins Publishers Ltd.

Text and illustrations copyright © Tony Ross 1999, 2001

The author/illustrator asserts the moral right to be identified as the author/illustrator of the work.

A CIP catalogue record for this title is available from the British Library.

The HarperCollins website address is: www.fireandwater.com

Printed in Hong Kong

I Want A Sister

Tony Ross

TED SMART

"There's going to be someone new in our family,"
said the Queen.

"Oh goody!" said the Little Princess.
"We're going to get a dog."

"No we're not," said the King.
"We're going to have a new baby."

"Oh goody!" said the Little Princess.
"I want a sister."

"It may be a brother," said the Doctor.
"You can't choose, you know."

"I don't want a brother," said the Little Princess.
"Brothers are smelly."

"So are sisters," said the Maid.
"Sometimes you smelled AWFUL."

"I don't want a brother," said the Little Princess.
"Brothers are rough."

"So are sisters," said the Admiral.
"Both make TERRIFIC sailors."

"I don't want a brother," said the Little Princess.
"Brothers have all the wrong toys."

"Brothers' toys can be just like yours,"
said the Prime Minister.

"Well," said the Little Princess,
"I JUST DON'T WANT A BROTHER."

"Why?" said everybody.
"BECAUSE I WANT A SISTER," said the Little Princess.

One day, the Queen went to the hospital
to have the new baby.
"Don't forget..." shouted the Little Princess,

"... I WANT A SISTER!"

"What if it's a brother?" said her cousin.

"I'll put it in the dustbin," said the Little Princess.

When the Queen came home from hospital,
the King was carrying the new baby.

"Say 'hello' to the new baby," said the Queen.
"Isn't she lovely?" said the Little Princess.

"He isn't a she," said the King. "You have a brother.
A little Prince!" "I don't want a little Prince,"
said the Little Princess. "I want a little Princess."

"But we already have a BEAUTIFUL little Princess,"
said the King and Queen.
"WHO?" said the Little Princess.

"YOU!" said the King and Queen.

"Can my brother have this,
now I'm grown up?"
said the Princess.

Collect all the funny stories featuring the demanding Little Princess!

0-00-662687-4

I Want My Potty
Tony Ross

"The Little Princess has huge appeal to toddlers and Tony Ross's illustrations are brilliantly witty."
Practical Parenting

0-00-664357-4

I Want To Be
Tony Ross

0-00-664356-6

I Want My Dinner
Tony Ross

0-00-664730-8

I Want A Sister
Tony Ross

0-00-710957-1

I Don't Want To Go To Hospital
Tony Ross

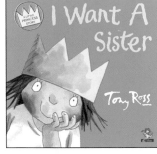

Tony Ross was born in London in 1938. His dream was to work with horses but instead he went to art college in Liverpool. Since then, Tony has worked as an art director at an advertising agency, a graphic designer, a cartoonist, a teacher and a film maker – as well as illustrating over 250 books! Tony, his wife Zoe and family live in Macclesfield, Cheshire.

Animals with Wings

Elizabeth Nonweiler

raintree

bee

mantid

thrip

cricket

comet moth

shark moth

queen ant

buzzard

red avadavat

ostrich

megabat

epomops bat

Interesting facts about the pictures

page 2: **Bees** have two pairs of wings which flap very fast to lift them up to fly from plant to plant. They take nectar from flowers and carry it back to their hives where they live with other bees.

page 3: **Mantids** have outer wings that look like leaves. These help them to hide from animals that eat them. They do not often use their wings for flying. Sometimes they spread them wide to frighten their enemies.

page 4: **Thrips** are tiny insects (up to 1 millimetre long). They have two wings, but they are not good at flying. Sometimes they are carried a long way by the wind. They feed on flowers and vegetables.

page 5: **Crickets** have wings with teeth-like combs on the bottom edges. They hold their wings open and run the top of one wing along the teeth at the bottom of the other wing to make chirping noises.

page 6: **Comet moths** come from the rainforests of Madagascar. They look like streaking comets when they fly. Moths begin life as caterpillars with no wings. They build a cocoon to stay in until their wings grow.

page 7: **Shark moths** live in grasslands, including roadside verges, and are common in England and Wales. Shark moth caterpillars like to eat thistles, but some moth caterpillars eat food crops and even clothes.

page 8: **Queen ants** have wings, but most ants are workers and do not have wings. A queen ant flies a long way to find a good place for a nest. Then she takes off her wings and starts producing eggs for new ants.

page 9: **Buzzards** can soar more than half a kilometre high into the sky on currents of air. They watch the ground with their excellent eyesight and then dive down to catch small animals such as rabbits to eat.

page 10: **Red avadavats** have beautiful red feathers. Their wings are black with white spots. They fly with rapid wingbeats and land in tall grass where they are difficult to see. They eat seeds and make nests with grass.

page 11: **Ostriches** are the biggest birds on Earth. They have wings, but they cannot fly. They can run very fast – up to 70 kilometres per hour. They live in grass and desert lands in Africa.

page 12: **Megabats** eat fruit, pollen and nectar. Microbats eat small animals and blood. All bats have wings formed by their digits (fingers) which are very long, spread out and joined by a thin skin, so they can fly.

page 13: **Epomops** are a type of megabat. This one has folded its wings around its body, while it hangs upside down to rest. Bats can grip with their feet without falling even when they are asleep.

Letter-sound correspondences

Level 1 books cover the following letter-sound correspondences.
Letter-sound correspondences highlighted in green can be found
in this book.

ant	big	cat	dog	egg	fish	get	hot	it
jet	key	let	man	nut	off	pan	queen	run
sun	tap	up	van	wet	box	yes	zoo	

duck	fish	chips	sing	thin this	keep	look moon	art	corn